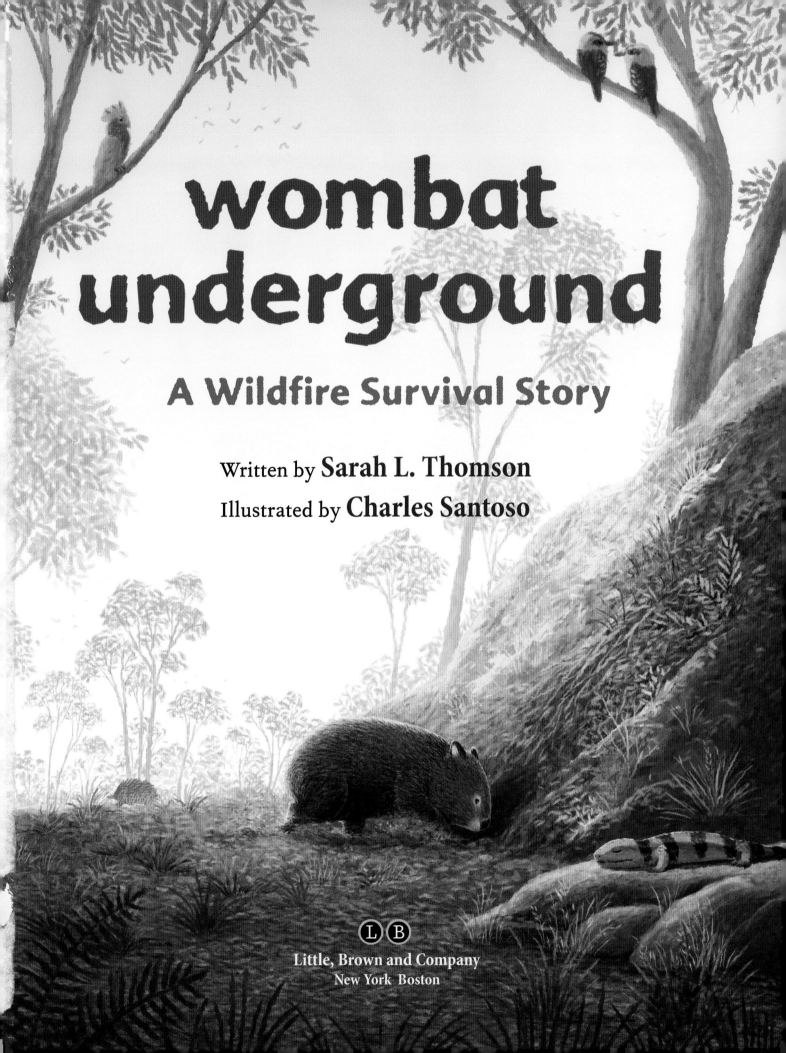

wombat underground

A Wildfire Survival Story

Written by **Sarah L. Thomson**

Illustrated by **Charles Santoso**

L B

Little, Brown and Company
New York Boston

Deep in the dirt
under the hill
roots grip tight
air is cool
water slips and drips

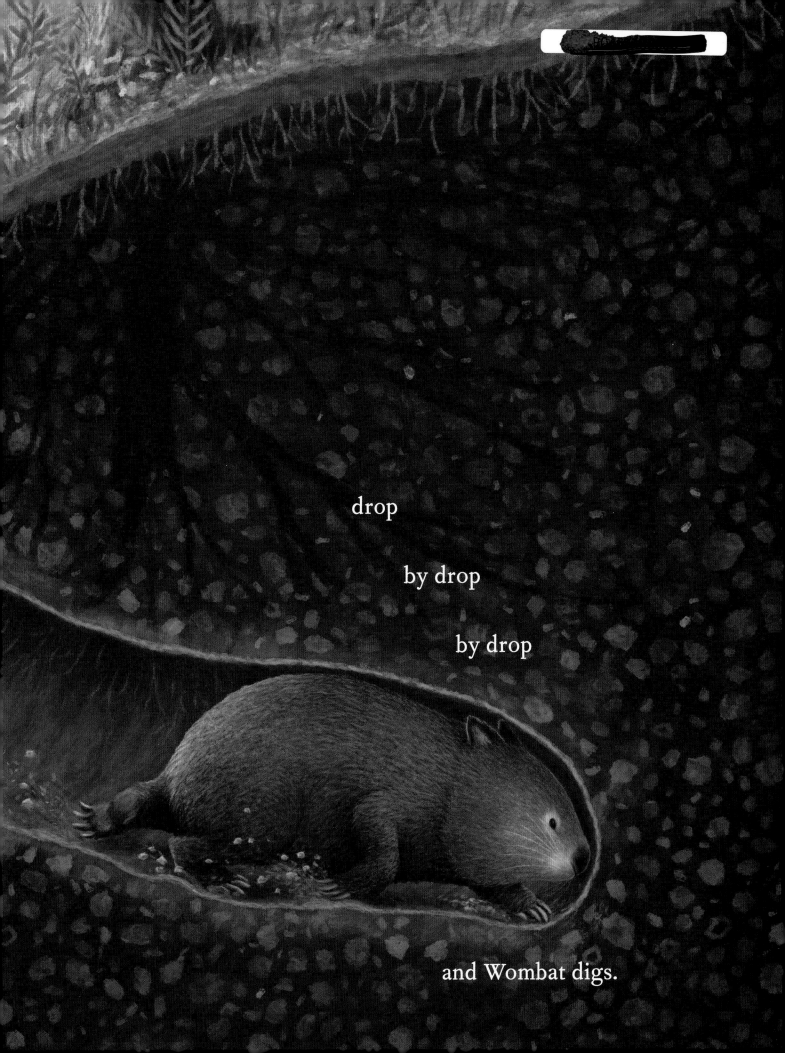

drop

by drop

by drop

and Wombat digs.

Up on the hill
Wallaby nibbles
leaves that burst with green.

Echidna listens
to grass that whispers
secrets of the wind.

Under the hill
Wombat carves out
a cave that's all his own.

Up on the hill
Skink dozes and dreams.
The sun beams down
and strokes her scales.

Deep in the dirt
the sun creeps in
and drinks all the water

drop

by drop

by drop.

Up on the hill
the sun beats down.
It shrivels the leaves
and steals all the green.

Skink slips
into the shade.

Wallaby licks
a puddle's last drop.

Echidna's grass
turns to rustling tinder
waiting for a match.

High in the sky
clouds boil and build.

Inside their billows
the match strikes and sparks.

Flakes of fire
sail on the wind.
Ribbons of smoke
snake through the grass.
Fingers of flame
claw up each tree.

Deep in the dirt
Wombat snorts and sleeps and snores.

Skink darts
from her shady spot.

Echidna runs
through blazing grass.

Wallaby bounds
over scorching coals.

Hot wind blows through Wombat's whiskers.
He blinks and stirs and wakes.

Scampering,

scurrying,

leaping,

loping,

animals flee toward the hole in the hill.

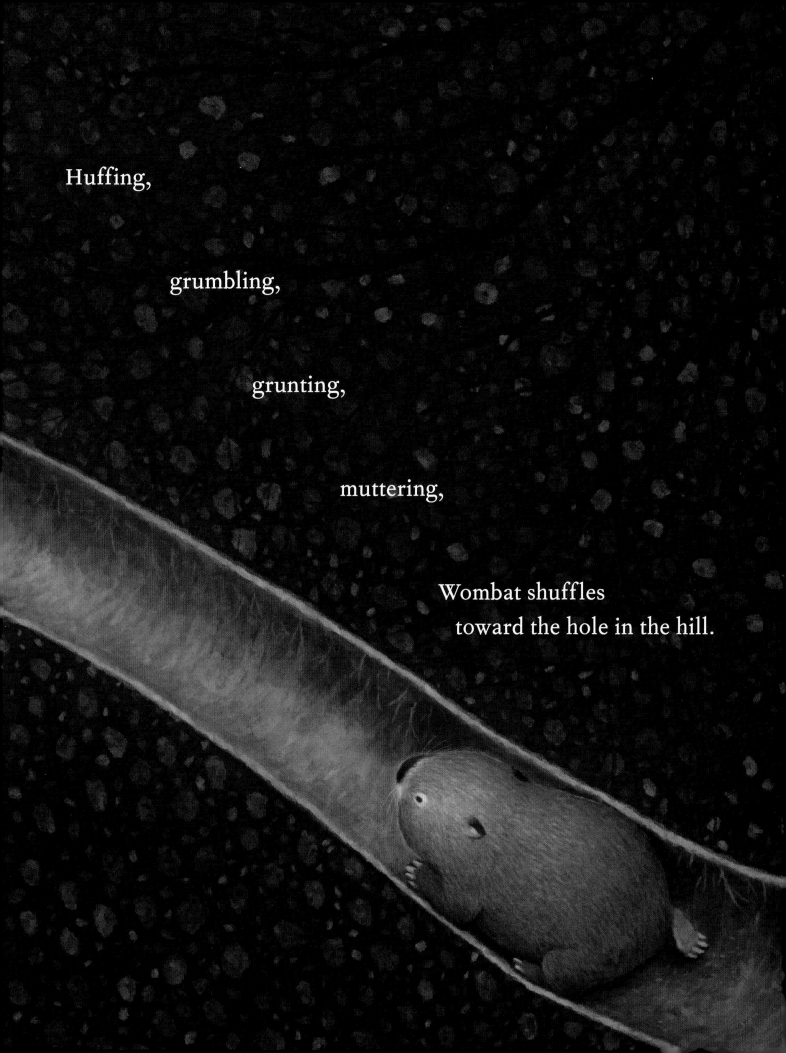

Huffing,

grumbling,

grunting,

muttering,

Wombat shuffles
toward the hole in the hill.

Trees are blazing.
Grass is burning.
Smoke is blinding.
Wombat is snarling,
ready to fight.

Claws that dig can scratch.
Teeth that bare can bite.
No stranger will enter
into the cave
he carved to be his own.

Skink hides stinging eyes.
Echidna limps on blistered feet.
Wallaby licks at blackened fur.

Fire is
the only enemy
here.

Step

by step

by step

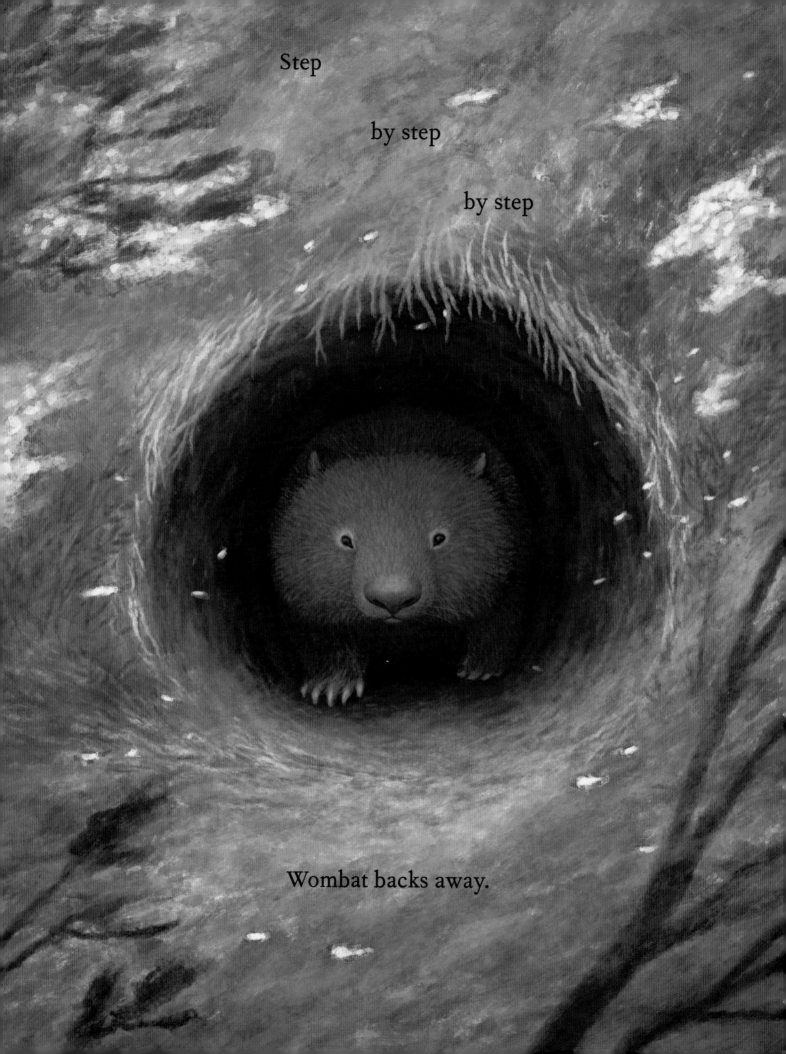

Wombat backs away.

Deep in the dirt
there is nothing to burn.

Under the hill
the creatures crowd in.

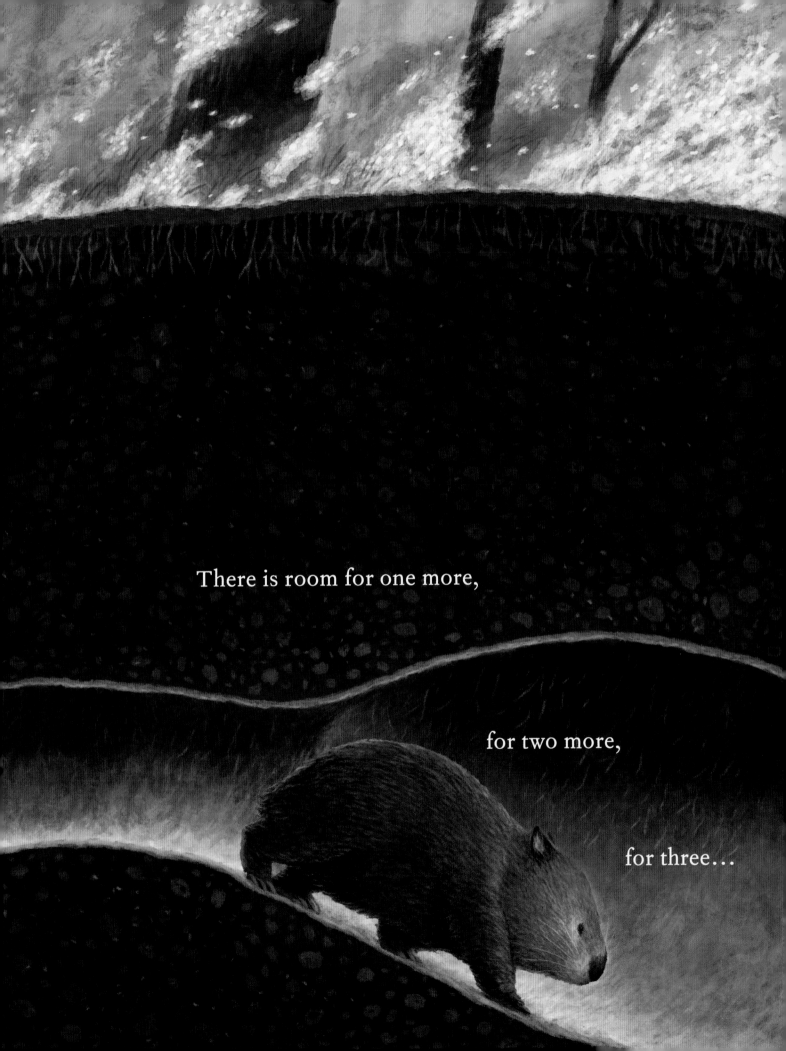

There is room for one more,

for two more,

for three...

room for us all

deep in the dirt

under the hill.

AUTHOR'S NOTE

Every year, Australia has a fire season. The north of the country is most at risk for wildfires, or bushfires, starting in winter and spring. In the south, the most dangerous time is in winter and autumn.

What starts the fires?

Many fires are started by lightning strikes. Other times people are to blame. They may start a fire by accident, maybe by tossing a lit cigarette, not putting out a campfire, or letting a spark fly from a piece of machinery. And a few fires have been set by people on purpose.

If the fires happen every year, are they really so bad?

Actually, small, regular bushfires are *good* for the wild landscape! They clear out dead, dry leaves and grass and wood. If small fires don't burn this tinder, it will pile up and lead to a huge fire later on. The ash from fires fertilizes soil and helps new plants grow. Some plants have seeds that need the heat of a fire to sprout. If there were no bushfires, these plants would die out. The trouble begins when bushfires don't stay small.

What made Australia's fires in 2019–2020 the worst in decades?

The world's climate has been slowly warming for years, which means that Australia has been getting hotter and drier. In 2019, temperatures reached 120 degrees Fahrenheit in some places.

The heat and the lack of rain dried out acres of leaves, grass, and wood. Once fires started, they burned so quickly that it was very difficult, or even impossible, for people to put them out. Some burned for months. By the time heavy rains doused the last of the flames, between twenty-four and forty million acres had burned—an area roughly the size of Iowa.

What happens to animals in a bushfire?

Some animals can flee. Some, like birds, can fly away. Some find refuge in water. And others can dig underground to stay safe. But not all animals survive. And if huge areas of grassland or forest are burned to ashes, the animals that make it through the fire still might starve.

No one knows exactly how many animals lost their lives or their habitats in the fire season of 2019–2020, but it's estimated that millions were killed, injured, or faced starvation. The Australian government has listed 119 animals who need special help to avoid extinction after the fires, including more than one species of echidna, wallaby, and skink.

What's an echidna? A wallaby? A skink?

An echidna is a small, spiny mammal that lays eggs. A wallaby is a marsupial (a mammal that carries its young in a pouch) that looks like a small kangaroo. Both are found naturally only in Australia and nearby islands. A skink is a kind of lizard. There are skinks all over the world, and several kinds are only found in Australia.

What about wombats?

They, too, are native to Australia and some surrounding islands. A wombat is a marsupial about the size of a golden retriever. They live in burrows that can have up to ninety yards of tunnels. When fires rage, these underground shelters become safe places, not just for wombats but for other creatures as well.

Wombats did not know it, but by doing what comes naturally to them— by digging—they saved the lives of many animals during the terrible fires of 2019–2020.

More About Wildfires

We Will Live in This Forest Again by Gianna Marino, Neal Porter Books, 2020

What Is a Bushfire? natgeokids.com/uk/discover/geography/physical-geography/what-is-a-bushfire

Wildfires by Kathy Furgang, National Geographic Kids, 2015

Wildfires by Seymour Simon, Collins, 2016

"*Wildfires.*" ready.gov/kids/disaster-facts/wildfires

More About Australian Animals

A Is for Australian Animals by Frané Lessac, Candlewick, 2018

"*Australia.*" kids.nationalgeographic.com/explore/countries/australia

"*Australian Animals.*" youtube.com/watch/TkCq54_ho-A

How to Scratch a Wombat: Where to Find It…What to Feed It…Why It Sleeps All Day by Jackie French and Bruce Whatley, Clarion Books, 2009

Super Marsupials: Kangaroos, Koalas, Wombats, and More by Katharine Kenah and Stephanie Fizer Coleman, HarperCollins, 2019

ABOUT THIS BOOK

The illustrations for this book were digitally done with Photoshop. This book was edited by Andrea Spooner and designed by Véronique Lefèvre Sweet and Christine Kettner. The production was supervised by Kimberly Stella, and the production editor was Annie McDonnell. The text was set in Fournier Mt Pro, and the display type is Advert Rough Pro.

For Linda —S.T.

For all fireys —C.S.